THESE KISSES ARE FOR:

Dixie Ubych :)

love aunty

lindsay xx

4 FLOWERS
3 BALLOONS

WHERE DO KISSES COME FROM?
YOU ASKED ME ONE DAY.
I TOLD YOU I GET THEM
FROM FAR, FAR AWAY.

THE FIRST KISS I FOUND HAD ESCAPED FROM THE ZOO.

I ran into more
when I went to Peru.

I gave them to you
and you asked me for more.

so I kept up my search
and headed offshore.

I GOT YOU
SOME KISSES

THAT FIT
IN A BOX,

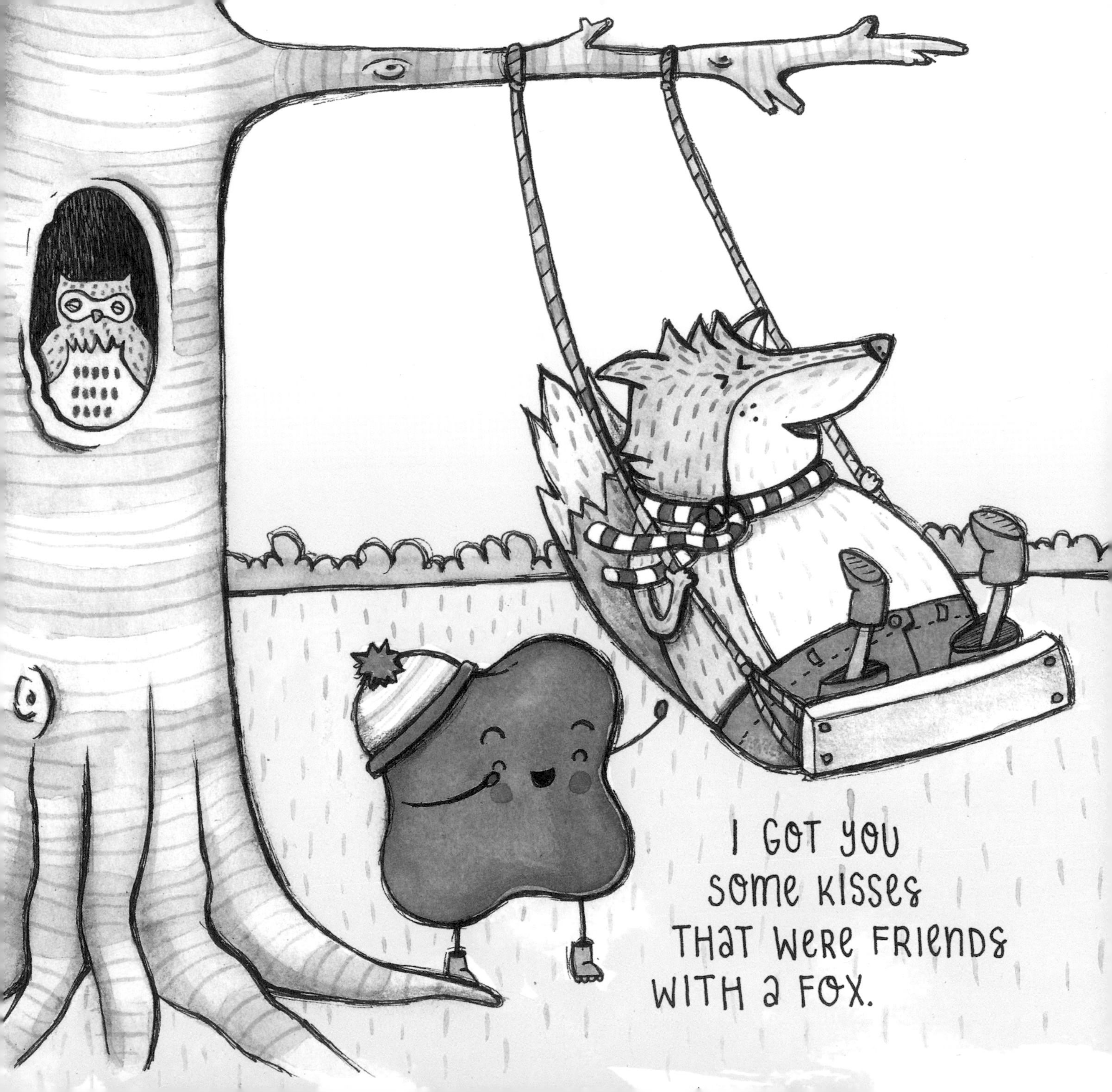

I GOT YOU
SOME KISSES
THAT WERE FRIENDS
WITH A FOX.

I got you some kisses
that gaze at the stars,

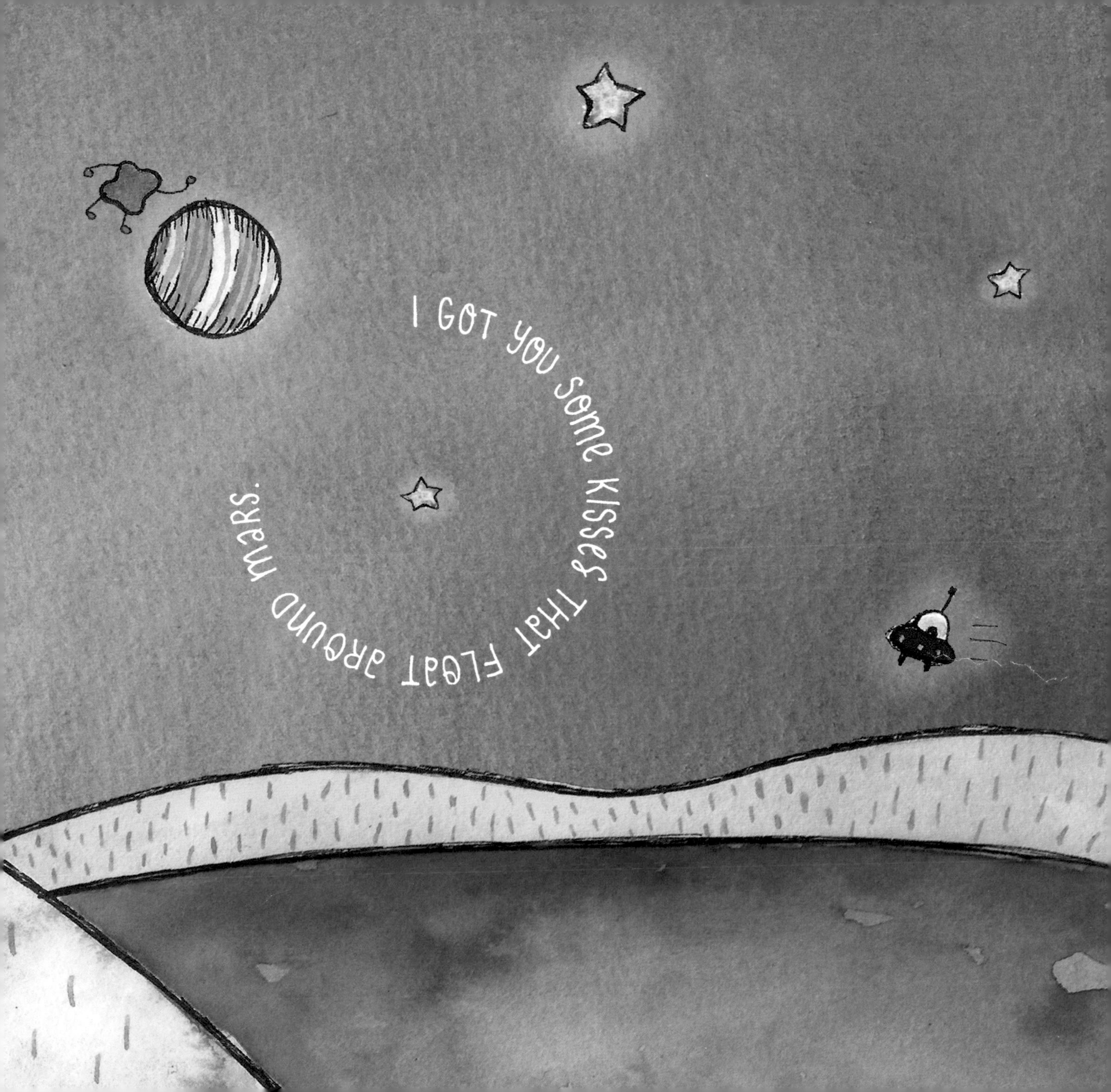
I GOT you some kisses That float around mars.

I GOT YOU SOME KISSES

WITH A COLLECTION OF HATS.

I GOT YOU SOME KISSES,
KISSING SIAMESE CATS!

I GOT YOU
SOME KISSES
ONE HAD
A PET SHOE,

I GOT YOU SOME KISSES,
ONE LOOKS JUST LIKE YOU!

One kiss I found
when collecting
the mail,

and these two I found,
simply do love to sail.

THIS KISS I FOUND HAD SNUCK IN MY POCKET.

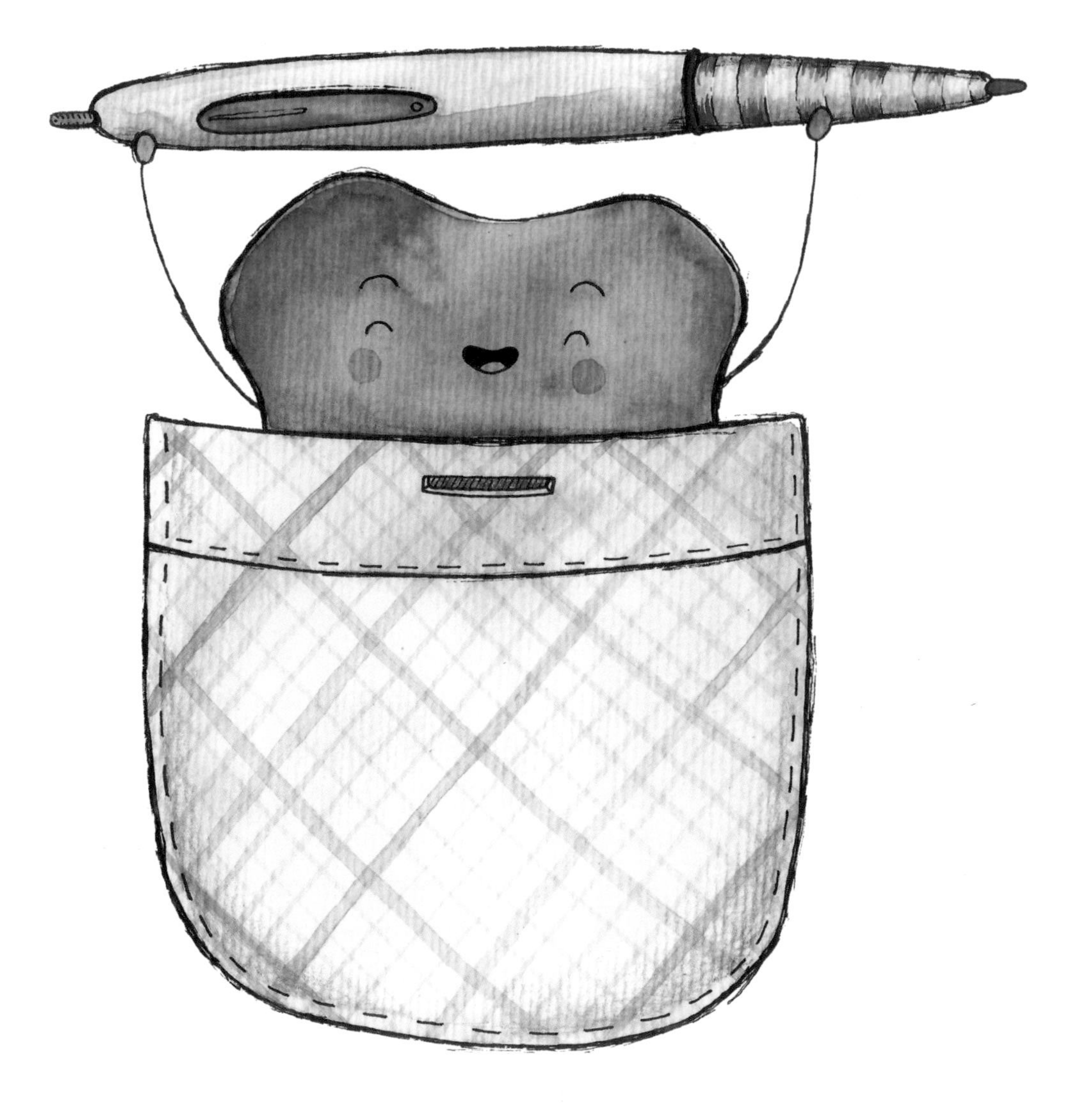

and this one, it seems, has arrived in a rocket.

THIS KISS, I FOUND HAVING TEA WITH A CUDDLE,

and THIS
one I FOUND
THINKS HIS HOUSE
IS a PUDDLE!

The kisses I find
come in all
shapes and sizes,

and sometimes
I find them in
silly disguises.

I GOT YOU
SOME KISSES,
FOR KISSING
YOUR TOES,

I GOT YOU
SOME KISSES
FOR KISSING
YOUR NOSE.

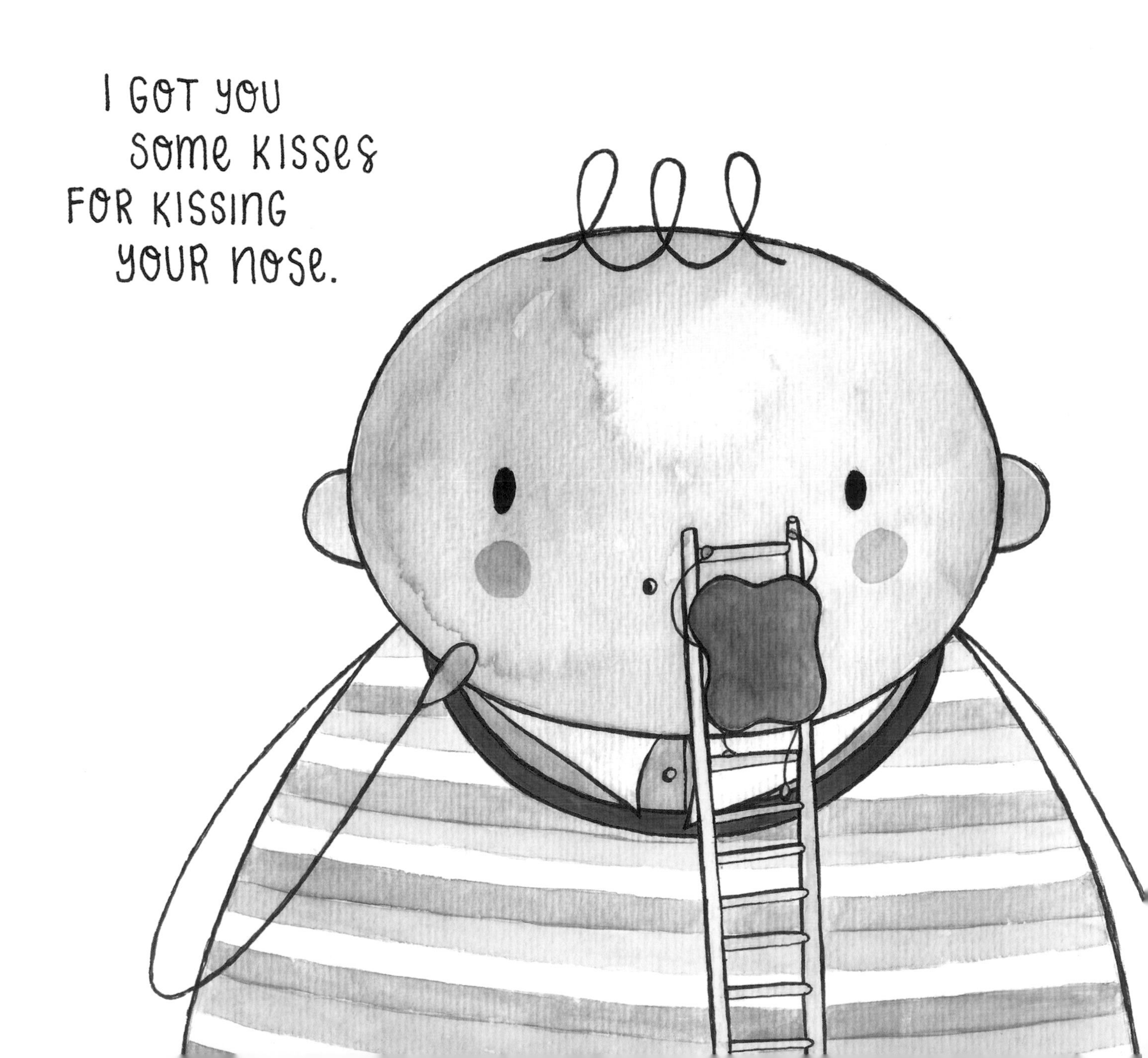

I GOT YOU
SOME KISSES,
TO HOLD
ON TO TIGHT,

I GOT YOU
SOME KISSES
TO KISS YOU
GOODNIGHT.

I GOT
YOU SOME KISSES,
WHO WILL SEEK WHEN
YOU HIDE.

I GOT YOU SOME KISSES TO BE BY YOUR SIDE.

now I've given you all
of the kisses I've got,

let's journey together
and find a new lot.